# INIQUITY

EMERY LEEANN

Iniquity

An Inferno World Novella

Emery LeeAnn

Iniquity Copyright 2019 by Emery LeeAnn
Inferno World Copyright 2017 by Yolanda Olson
Cover Design by Dez Purington of Pretty in Ink Creations
Edited and Formatted by Ed Bar

FOREWORD

Welcome to Hell.

In this place of darkness, the weak are easily consumed, and those brave enough to fight are served on a silver platter for the devils that have stolen them.

They eyes of those that watch are the ones that should be feared the most. The need to feel disgusting and repulsive are granted with a smile, but only for those that obey his every command.

Have you come to do the devil's work along with the one who longs for the devil's touch?

There is no hope here.

Only pain.

Only suffering.

Only death for the wicked.

## FOREWORD

Iniquity is going to break your heart, but that's what you came for isn't it?

To see how far Hell can reach and if you can survive its grasp?

Get ready to fucking burn.

Yolanda Olson

*When you dive into my little piece of Inferno World, think of the Queen of Horror herself, to whom I am dedicating this book, Yolanda Olson. Without her book, Inferno, this would never have come to fruition. She has been a consummate cheerleader the whole way for me, even when I wanted to hide! Love this bitch to pieces!*

# 1

## EVE

Have you ever felt sad? For no reason at all, or for every reason, your mind cannot decide. You are happier than you have ever been, yet so miserable. Your mind knows something must be fucked up.

Yeah, that was my existence. My goal was to make him proud of me on some level, any level, really. I just wanted him to know that I was worthy of his redemption. Because in the end, that was what he did. He delivered me from evil and redeemed my soul.

But I am getting ahead of myself. Let me start from the beginning. Who was he? He was my stepbrother, Luke. His father apparently had a fling with my mother after she was already pregnant with me. I didn't even know of his existence until he approached me at the playground that day.

My mom was a junkie. She would do anything for a quick fix. Including taking the food right out of my mouth to pay for her filthy habit. She had no issues with locking me in the closet while she paraded men in and out of our dingy, little apartment, letting them use her body so that she could earn her junk. The sound of her grunting and moaning, as man after man shot their load inside her, still rang heavily in my ears at night.

If she was not able to get her daily dose of junk, then I took the brunt of it, and it could be very bad at times. I became her punching bag from the moment I learned to walk; black eyes and bruised ribs became the norm for me. Her way of apologizing was letting me go to the abandoned park right outside our rundown building to be a normal kid, or at least as much of a normal kid that my deprived mind could imagine. The visits to the park, however, were not entirely out of generosity, nor were it an actual apology. The visits to the park were also an easy opportunity for her to score some more blow.

One day, I noticed someone watching us from the corner of the building. I could barely see out of my right eye because it was swollen from her punching me in the face after a man dashed out without paying for the pleasure of her pussy, so I didn't get a real good look at the stranger. So I just thought it was one of her hook-ups. There was always someone hanging around the park, trying to buy or sell dope, so it was not unusual to see someone shady looking.

I walked over to the slide and started up the steps, one by one, as he walked closer to Momma. When he sat down beside her, you could just sense the atmosphere change. My mom sat up straighter, as rigid as a plank of wood, looking almost scared for a moment, but then seemed to calm down some. He bent down and whispered something in her ear. She looked downright stricken from whatever it was that he had said to her. He sat back and smiled the most menacing, alarming smile that I had ever seen in my young life. At this point, presently in my life, I would kill for that smile, but back then, it scared the living bejeezus out of me. I could feel the cold drip of fear seeping through my body. He looked over at me as I sat at the top of the slide, nodded his head, got up, and walked away. Gripped by an unexplainable terror, I froze in my spot, unable to do anything except blink as I watched his menacing figure disappear into a crowd of passersby.

Momma yelled my name. I slid down the slide and walked slowly over to her with a different sense of apprehension. Somehow, I knew that I was in trouble. As usual, I didn't know why. I just knew that I was.

Thwack. Her hand crashed into my mouth, and the familiar sting spread over my face. The iron tang of the blood from my freshly busted lip saturated my taste buds.

"What did I do, Momma?" I cried, staring at her dumbfounded through wide, bewildered eyes.

"The sins of your stepfather just came back to haunt me, and I'll be damned if that demon spawn of his will threaten me about my own child." She grabbed me by my hair and dragged me across the asphalt. My scalp burned as she led me back into our apartment building.

I was still confused as to what she was talking about when she shoved me in the cramped, little closet. I tried to get as comfortable as I could, knowing that she would most likely leave me in there overnight.

I had never seen my mother so nervous. She had always been at least a little twitchy because of her habit, but now, she was downright shaking in fear. Part of me had been curious, but the other part of me just wanted to be able to go to sleep without her hitting me again. Any time I could avoid a punch to the face was a blessing.

After dozing off for what only seemed like a few

minutes, I woke up to my mom screaming at someone to get out. Rubbing my eyes, I sat up in the closet just as the door swung open. The stranger stood there with his hand held out. Peering out around him, I saw my mother sprawled out on the ratty, little couch that she slept on. She looked like she was still breathing. Actually, she looked like she was in a deep and peaceful slumber, but I knew that I had heard her screaming just a few minutes before.

I could remember the timid nature of my reaching for his hand. Now, I begged for his touch. He waited for me to stand up, and then, he pulled me out of the closet.

"Did she do that to your mouth after I left today?" He asked, gently tracing the swollen laceration on my bottom lip.

I nodded my head as if to say yes. He cursed under his breath. "I told her to never touch you again or there would be consequences."

Cocking my head to the left, I had to ask, "Who are you?"

"Luke," he answered tersely, "I'm your stepbrother, and I'm taking you away from here. Right now."

"Are you kidnapping me?" I asked, surprised, but not exactly hating the idea, despite his intimidating stature and the visible anger etched on his face.

"Unless you would rather stay here," he grunted, shrugging his shoulders noncommittingly.

"No, I want to go with you." I ignored the slowly creeping fear that had consumed me earlier on the slide. There was nothing but pain and neglect for me here. At least he had shown some concern over my wellbeing.

He nodded as if he knew that he was my only choice. My mom groaned on the couch. He looked at her, handed me a knife, and said, "You need to learn how to dispose of the malignancies that give you pain." He gave me a wicked smile. "This is your first lesson on learning what it means to be in a real family. I want you to slice her throat open with this knife."

Looking at him, I was not sure if he was serious or not. My hand was shaking as I held the knife. I was not sure which was more surreal, the act of killing my mother or that I was taking orders from a stranger who claimed to be my stepbrother, and doing it willingly. My feet acted of their own accord, carrying me across the linoleum, even as my mind warred with itself. Could I kill my own mother? The woman who gave me life?

The woman who systematically stripped me of my innocence, one slap, punch and kick at a time?

The distance from the closet to the couch seemed to stretch for miles, every step I took felt as if it moved me farther away. My hand trembled, the sharp point of the blade wobbling as it directed me. I had never thought about taking a life before. How could I do it? What would it mean? What would it say about me as a person? My conscience screamed at me as I approached, but there was a darkness in my soul that washed it away with whispering words of encouragement. No longer would she be able to hurt me. No longer would she be able to trap me in the darkness that had permeated my very being. Now that darkness was my freedom. He was my freedom.

All I had to do was press the blade against the soft flesh of her neck and then slide it.

I stood over Momma's prone body, watching her chest rise and fall with each breath that she took. Her eyes roamed under their lids, and I took a moment to ponder what she might be dreaming. Was she having a nightmare of her child hovering above her, slowly moving the blade to her throat? A part of me hoped that she was. Her waking nightmare would be her closet. All I needed to do was to shut and lock the door, and then she would be trapped in her torment for eternity. I tightened my grip on the handle, steadying my nerves, if not my limbs. My fingers tensed, and I looked up at him for approval.

He nodded his head, a slow-spreading smile stretching his lips. I tilted my mom's head back so that I could have access to her throat. She was snoring lightly, no doubt still high off her last fix. My hand shook like crazy, as I slid the knife across her throat in a jagged line. Droplets of blood bubbled up in the crevice of the cut and trickled down her neck to her throat, forming a shallow pool in the hollow above her collarbone. She was starting to wake up from the pain, her eyes struggling to open under the blanket of dope.

I felt an insurmountable sense of exhilaration wash over me as I watched her, lying beneath me helpless. It was a marvelous thing to witness our sudden role-reversal, but I expected more. More blood, more of a fight, more…something.

"You did a good job…" I beamed at his praise. "…but…" Wait, he said but. "…you need to do it again, and press harder on the knife so that it slices clear through the flesh." He smiled encouragingly.

I sighed loudly, not because he wanted me to do it again but because I didn't get it right the first time. I didn't know why, but I wanted to be perfect for him. I put the blade back to her neck and started to drag the tip with more pressure when her arms flew up to stop me. He very casually grabbed her by the wrists, put his legs on top of them to hold them above her head, and used his hand to help me apply more pressure. I felt the difference as I cut through the meaty part of her throat, but I felt something else as well, a spark that ignited from his touch. A spark that spread through my body like wildfire through brush. The blood was drenching her shirt as she gurgled, failing in her attempt to breathe. We stayed there, his hand over mine, until she took her last wet, ragged breath.

"Good job." He smiled what I would learn was a rare, warm smile. A smile that I would crave. A smile that would drive me to do anything to receive. "This is the first lesson you needed. You did great. What's your name?"

"Evelyn," I replied with a grimace, the realization of what I had just done hitting me. I just took a life. Not just any life, but the life of the woman who gave me mine. The life of a woman who had tormented me. I swallowed down the emotional whirlwind wreaking havoc in my stomach. I could deal with that later. All I wanted in that moment was his approval.

"It will be Eve from now on. And your forbidden apple…well, that will be your loyalty to me and how much you can handle to be part of an actual family."

I didn't know what he was referring to by the apple reference, but my lessons, I would soon learn, would rip the very fiber of my being, taking me to new heights of terror, pain, and ecstasy. I would soon find out that he wanted to create the perfect monster, so I would surrender my soul to give him one. After all, a monster had tormented me, and a monster had saved me.

Luke, my stepbrother, would own every ounce of my humanity, and I would beg for more. It was the welcome to being a part of a real family.

## 2

### EVE

Getting to the house that I would now live in was scary. We walked for what seemed like an eternity. In hindsight, I was sure that it was only a couple of blocks or so, before we reached his vehicle. I fell asleep on the ride to his house, physically, mentally and emotionally exhausted by what I had just done.

Luke was my guardian angel in my mind, until I saw the darkness in his stare. His eyes had a way of sinking right into your soul, ripping out your deepest, darkest, secrets. I am not sure at which point that I knew that I had left my undeniable destruction only to end up in my own personal hell. Whatever the reasoning, the universe had brought Luke into my life for better or worse. No matter what abuse that I incurred, I would never want to change a single thing.

Throughout the years, Luke trained me to be as lethal as he was. As his sister, he explained, I was special, so he would train me himself. As my lessons went on throughout the years, I found that my brother was evil incarnate, my own personal devil, and that I was his perfect sacrifice. He was using me as a test subject, if you will. A macabre experiment. He wanted to see how much one person could endure without utterly shattering to pieces. The thing that he didn't count on was that I welcomed the abuse. I looked forward to the pain. I craved his torture. Was it wrong that I wanted him to peel my flesh piece by piece, strip by strip, sliver by sliver, while he ravaged me body and soul? My only purpose, as far as I was concerned, was to please Luke and make him proud of me. His gratification was my only concern. And I would sacrifice anyone or anything to make that happen. If he bade me to eat the heart of an infant while he forced its father to fuck me with a cock drenched in its dying mother's blood, then I would do it over and over. I would systematically go from house to house, from neighborhood to neighborhood, until organs filled my belly and bloody semen filled my womb.

3

EVE

WHEN MY BROTHER first took my virginity, it was cold and without emotion. As much as I tried to give him the same back, I failed when the tears began rolling down my cheeks. He finished his business with a deep, guttural grunt and then rolled off me. He told me to go shower and get myself cleaned up. I obeyed him without question, and the shower helped, washing away my tears. He was waiting in the bathroom with a towel when I pulled the shower curtain back. He explained that the physical act of sex would not be for my gratification until I learned how to do it the right way and please him properly. It was another lesson that my pleasure was only an extension of his; that I was to be an extension of him. I needed to figure out how to deal with it without getting emotional. After all, he saved me from my hideous mother, did he not? He was right. He was my salvation, and I owed him nothing less. This was the very least that I could do to show my appreciation, to make sure that his needs were taken care of.

So I learned how to endure his physical needs of my body. It was my curse for being a female, and his right for being my savior. But as a female, getting older, my body was starting to have needs too. I would always be his sister first, but I was still a woman. The more practice that I got, the more my body responded. I learned when to move and how to move. My mind still hadn't caught up though. I cried every single time, which pissed him off. One day he broke the mold and flipped me over on top of him, so that I could ride him. My body betrayed me, or maybe it didn't, and moved in ways that my mind was not able to conjure. My hips rocked and gyrated, bouncing up and down in a rhythm never before known to me. My body fucked his like a wild banshee, and I took every inch of stiff cock that he offered. I milked every drop of semen that exploded from his throbbing shaft. I came harder than I ever had before. My orgasm shook the very foundation of my being. My eyes were watery. When I felt him pinch my nipples hard and twist them, my eyes opened wide, tears spilling out over my cheeks. I looked down at him and then shrunk back from his look of disgust.

"You cry like I'm hurting you, but your pussy is telling a different story."

I tried to make it up to him, but it was too late. Maybe he had unrealistic expectations, but he was not wrong. He could never be wrong. The fault was mine for not being perfect for him. I would just have to try harder. He slammed my face down into the mattress, holding me there. I felt the leather strap come down across my back again and again, lash after lash. Family did not lie to family, and in his mind, I was trying to deceive him by saying that I didn't enjoy him fucking me. And it was true, at least physically, that I enjoyed every thrust of his magnificent cock. I was only struggling with the inexperience of my mind, coming to grips with what was happening to me. He was brutal when he took my body, and I did enjoy it, but I also knew that if he knew how much I craved the physical pleasure, that information would also make him angry. He needed to make the decisions, not me. It was never meant to be about me or my needs, nor should it be about me or my cravings. My entire existence was solely for his pleasure. I was made for him. I didn't see that as some sort of injustice, but as a goal that I needed to work toward, and the sooner the better, for both of us. And every time that I did not live up to that goal, I was the only one to blame. It just meant that I had to work harder. I had to fuck for his pleasure, not mine, and swallow any residue of adolescent purity that still infected the deep recesses of my mind. I had to be his fuck toy. I wanted to be his fuck toy. I needed his approval, his rare smile of pride. And I hated myself whenever I screwed things up and denied both of us his pleasure.

His darkness eventually leaked into me. He didn't trust anyone, so I had to look for the deceit in everyone. Nobody was your ally but your family. At best, they were your pawns, and at worst, they were your rivals, but mostly they were a means for your sadistic pleasure. Learning this was harsh and brutal, but learn it, I did. It took several beatings to have this ingrained in my mind, beatings that I willingly accepted. Unlike when Momma used to beat me, these were for my own good. They were the vehicle that would drive me forward and let me grow. Though, I believed that I had learned that lesson the first time, he knew that he needed to remind me frequently, and I tried never to argue with him. He was always right.

My love of pain came from these sessions. I found that cutting my skin was especially stimulating for me. It helped me to let my demons out when the stress started to get too much for me to take. Just cutting the thick meaty flesh of my upper thigh and watching the blood stream down was almost like an aphrodisiac. Watching the blood run down my legs could easily put me into a hypersexual trance.

One specific time came easily to mind. I sat on the bedroom floor, feeling neglected after he stormed off out of anger. I was still struggling with my stupid tears, and he had had just about enough. Once he was gone, I crawled over to a recently discarded knife and began slicing, each new cut accelerating my arousal. It was wrong of me, but I began touching myself with my free hand, twisting my nipples and slapping my face, seeing Luke in my mind's eye. I let my fingers trail down my torso, my nails digging into my flesh, leaving long, red marks in their wake. I slid a finger inside of me, pushing it as deep as it would go, pressing down on my clit with my thumbnail, as I slid the blade along my thigh once more. I began thrusting, dropping the knife as I tilted my head back, imagining my brother on top of me, claiming me, taking me hard. I traced my fingers through my blood and put them in my mouth. I sucked them clean as I began thrusting harder, curling my finger. There were no tears. Why could I not accomplish this when he fucked me?

Thankfully, I heard him approaching before he opened the door, and he caught me in my pleasure. I was fearful of how he would have reacted if he had witnessed me seeking it without him.

When he saw me sitting in a puddle of my own blood, he picked up the knife. Without a word, he cut a strip of skin from my right hip, never losing eye contact. The tip of the blade cut a smooth line, and then another, with the points connecting. He peeled away the strip of loose flesh and tossed it to the floor. The sting of pain filled me, driving me over the precipice of climax, and I had a mini orgasm. My slight moan of gratification did not escape him. He looked down at me in disgust and then turned and walked back out of the room, taking the knife with him. I think it was at this point that he began to lose interest in me.

My goal was to make him proud, so that he would love me again. I wanted to make a grand gesture, something to show my dedication to him. I did this later that night. While he was lying in bed, his arms folded behind his head, staring up at the ceiling, lost in thought, I walked in, holding a tube of super glue. I was determined to keep the tears back. I stopped at the edge of the bed and unscrewed the cap. I carefully slid the tip across my eyes, first the left and then the right, lightly squeezing the tube. I only had to wait seconds before my eyes were sealed shut. There would be no way that my tears could escape.

I climbed up on the bed, feeling my way over to him. When my hand landed on his chest, I smiled. "Take me. I want to please you. I won't cry. I'll be perfect, I promise. You will be pleased."

I immediately knew that it was a mistake. My voice was too whiny. I sounded too needy. I didn't need to have my sight in order to know that he was glaring at me angrily. I felt pressure on my wrist, and I felt his chest way under my fingers. The darkness spun, and I landed on my back. A gasp blew past my lips, and then his fist landed on them. The bitter taste of pennies filled my mouth.

"Have I taught you nothing?" he asked in a deep, breathless growl. His index fingers and thumbs pinched my eyelids. I knew what was coming, so I braced myself for the ensuing pain. Keeping a tight grip on the two thin flaps of flesh, he yanked upward. My eyelids ripped open, blood droplets forming at every one of the multitude of tiny lacerations. "You control your emotions. You will never take shortcuts. Do you understand me?"

I nodded reverently, staring up at his blurry visage.

The pain that spread through me and gripped my

nervous system was far more intense than simply cutting my legs. It was on a whole new level, and, in my dark, demented way, I enjoyed it so much more than a simple blade slicing my skin. I choked back the involuntary gasp, ready to show him that I could be a master over my emotions, and controlling my reaction to pain was much easier than controlling my incessant crying any day of the week.

"Turn over," he barked. "I can't look at your pathetic face."

I would be lying if I said that my heart didn't break a little, but I did as he commanded, as I always did. I buried my bloody face into the pillow as he straddled the backs of my thighs. To show me what true mastery of self looked like, he rested his limp cock between my ass cheeks. Without a single thrust, using no friction to draw blood into his organ, it began to grow, thickening, hardening.

He drove his dry, throbbing shaft deep into my ass without hesitation. I bit back a scream. I was not expecting anal, but I should have known that his twisted mindset would see that as the ultimate punishment for what he saw as my betrayal.

His hips pressed firmly into my ass cheeks, his cock deep inside of me. He wrapped his hand in my hair and yanked my head back. "You will not let the pillow hide your tears. If I see a single, salty drop, I will go get my bat and ass-fuck you with it until it splinters inside of you."

My addiction to pain almost made me want to shed some tears. Almost. This was not about my pain, just as it was not about my pleasure. It was about living for him, letting him use me. So I laid there and took his assault without so much as a whimper, and for the first time since he rescued me, I did not cry.

---

No one and no thing was safe around us. Everything that Luke did, he taught me to do. I showed great skill in hunting. People and animals, they were the same thing to us. There were woods outside of our house. I found myself alone more frequently, so I needed something to kill the time, and nothing killed time like killing. I began to take daily walks through the trees. I quickly became familiar with my surroundings, memorizing every natural and manmade landmark, a rock in the shape of a crooked arrow, several fallen trees and every path that twisted around the property. These were my hunting grounds. Here, I was a natural predator.

Deciding to set some traps, I thought that maybe I could catch dinner for us one night. I was a survivalist junkie, watching all the documentaries that I could find on being able to survive in the wilderness. Anything that would improve my skills. Luke always reminded me that he might leave me for good at some point. That thought always made me physically ill, but I had to plan for what he promised would be inevitable. But I had to admit that the thought of not having him there, touching me, whether it was harsh or not, teaching me, guiding me, made me want to vomit. I felt as if I would wither away and die without him in my life.

Who would I be without him? He trained me to be his extension, to be a part of him. Leaving me on my own was a fate crueler than anything else that he could ever do to me.

I went to check on my traps, and there was a rabbit caught in its clutches. It looked at me with its little black eyes. I could feel its pain in their depths, and I wondered if this was how Luke felt when he looked at me. I picked it up, releasing it from the trap and held it in my arms. The animal was shivering with fright and shaking in pain. I was so excited to get an animal that I almost dropped it as it twitched, jerked and tried to jump away.

"Oh, no you don't, little one."

I grabbed it by the neck and twisted it until I heard a small crack. I held it up by its twisted neck in one hand, and wrapped my other hand around its body. I squeezed as firmly as I could and slid my hand down its torso. I could feel its insides squishing, its bones cracking and splintering. Bloody clumps of organs and tissue exploded out of its ass. I am not sure that I had ever had a bigger smile on my face than when I had my first successful kill. Reaching for my pocketknife, so that I could skin it and field dress it properly, I became suddenly pissed off at myself. I forgot it or lost it, because my pocket was empty. My hand grasped nothing but air.

Looking down at the small animal in my hand, I sat down and wondered why I could not simply use my hands. Sure, it would not be as clean or efficient, but it would get the job done. In my head, my hands and my teeth were my biggest weapons. Those were things you could not lose or forget. In the end, a predator did not need a knife for such trivial things.

I flipped the animal on its back. It was too mangled and deflated to make sense of, let alone for me to skin without any tools. I would have to rethink my position on this. As luck would have it, another fat one was in the other trap. This one was in a cage, unlike the first trap that had snared the rabbit by one of its hind legs. This rabbit hadn't felt the sting of a broken leg. It didn't tremble in fear or shake with pain. It sat safely behind its wired cage, watching me with curious eyes, unaware of its fate.

I was excited to see how this would work.

I knelt down next to it and studied it, smiling at the friendly looking creature. Its fur was a blend of varying shades of gray. Its wide eyes seemed almost trusting of my intentions, as if it were waiting for me to free it from its imprisonment. I loved its sense of innocence. I loved that I was about to exploit it. It filled me with a sense of gratification that I had yet ever to experience. I would soon have that feeling again, only heightened, but at this point, it was exhilarating. As I pulled it out of the cage, the furry, little guy tried to jump away as the other rabbit had, but I held on to him tightly around his body. He would not escape. He was mine.

"What are you doing?"

A scrawny skit of a girl was peering at me from around a tree. "I am going to skin this animal." I shrugged, as if it was not obvious by my holding on to the wriggling animal that no longer felt safe in my presence.

"What are you doing that for?"

She was starting to annoy me. "Do you want something? What is your name?"

"Mercy. My name is Mercy. And, yeah, I wanna

watch as you skin that rabbit." She looked at me expectantly.

I looked at the wonder on her face and shrugged. "Then sit down and be quiet, Mercy. Not a single peep. Is that understood?"

She nodded as if to say yes. She didn't wait for me to agree to let her watch. Instead, she scooted over toward me until I glared at her, which made her freeze, sitting as still as she could. Flipping over Roger, that was my name for all rabbits, I put him in between my legs, laying him on his back. He peered up at me with his soulful eyes and twitchy nose, trying his hardest with his tiny, little brain to comprehend what was happening to him. Positioning my thumbs in between his breastbone, I pushed as hard as I could until I felt the fur give way and my thumbnail sink into his soft flesh. His thrashing was making it hard to hold him still, so I pulled my bloody thumb out of his body and then twisted his neck. Like the previous rabbit, the small bones cracked and popped and then, finally, he was still.

Digging my fingers back into the hole that I made, stretching it to fit both of my index and middle fingers, I pulled as hard as I could. At first, there was no give, but then the hole stretched further. I pulled the carcass up to my mouth and sank my teeth into it. I yanked and chewed until the growing hole became a jagged slit. I kept at it, and the slit stretched up to its throat, and down past its belly. The rabbit's innards flopped out and plopped to the ground. I pulled the skin from the body. Grabbing each of its limbs one by one, I yanked them from inside their furry casing. The fur hung from the rabbit's neck, leaving its pale red body exposed, pot marked with the bits of fur that remained. I could see the muscles and tendons beneath the mucus exterior.

I was concentrating so hard that I completely forgot about the girl sitting beside me until she sucked in a deep breath. I directed my gaze at her and she backed away, looking, no pun intended, like a scared rabbit.

"Did you know that when you look at people, you look like a killer? Your eyes are cold and lifeless." She quivered.

Shrugging again, "I didn't invite you to watch, so you are more than welcome to leave."

"I would like to stay, please," she whispered, intent on seeing this through.

I shrugged noncommittingly. It's her funeral.

The fur was too tough to pull off its head with just my hands. I cocked my head as I studied it. I thought for a moment before I realized what I needed to do.

I looked over at the girl. "Mercy, it's time for you to go home now. Don't tell anyone that you met me, okay? If you want to come out at the same time tomorrow, I will be here."

The girl looked like she wanted to argue, but she was too scared, so she jumped to her feet and then ran away, in a zigzag pattern until she disappeared. Satisfied that she was gone and would not be coming back anytime soon, I knelt down and searched for a rock with a somewhat sharp edge to it. It took a moment, but I eventually found one that seemed suitable for my purposes. I could still taste dirt and blood from using my teeth. Smacking my lips with a slight grin, I used my teeth to hold on to one edge of the fur, and pulled at the other with my free hand. I began sawing at it with the rock. It was a slower process than I believed it would have been, but eventually I made enough leeway to loosen it around the rabbit's neck. It was a raw and primal feeling, tasting the animal's death as I mutilated its fur. I let go of it with my mouth and dropped the rock. Gripping its slimy body with one hand and its fur with the other, I yanked as hard as I could in several quick successions, and I finally pulled the fur free from the rabbit. Feeling accomplished, I tossed the hide to the ground.

"That was awesome," Mercy squealed.

Whirling my head around, I saw her hiding behind a tree. Shaking my head in annoyance, I ignored her. Its tiny, lifeless heart was still wedged in its chest cavity. I needed to finish gutting the animal, and take it home for a stew. I was really looking forward to reap the rewards of my kill.

"Can I have the fur?" Mercy asked.

I bent down, snatched up the hide, and threw it at her. Her glee had me smiling in spite of myself. "Now go home for real," I demanded of her.

"See you tomorrow," the girl practically sang as she skipped away.

4

EVE

I WAS DELIGHTED when I saw that there was a light on through the kitchen window. It meant that I would not be eating dinner alone. I was hoping this would make him happy. I walked in with a smile on my face. Unfortunately, I forgot about my disheveled appearance. The look of disdain on his face pierced me like a shard of glass sliding into my heart.

I handed him the carcass, feeling guilty for not planning ahead and cleaning up. He told me to go take a shower. I did as he bid, and after I closed the bathroom door, I looked into the mirror. I saw the dried dirt and blood all over my face, caked around my mouth. I looked horrible. No wonder he was disgusted; I was disgusted with myself. I needed to start thinking before I acted. Just because you can use your teeth, does not mean you should. Another lesson learned.

I turned on the hot water faucet, ignoring the cold. The scolding hot water would do me good. There must always be a price to be paid for my infractions. I would accept the molten-hot water and let it burn away my neglectfulness. I hopped into the steam-filled shower, fighting the urge to jump back out, and scrubbed myself clean. My skin was beet red when I finally stepped out and dried myself off. I flinched as I imagined his anger over the appearance of flesh, but prayed that he would see it as my penance for causing him displeasure. I went into the bedroom and put on clean clothes.

I came down after I finished getting dressed; double checking to make sure that I was squeaky clean, to find out that he was gone. Again. He left dinner cooking, the rabbit stew that I had intended to cook for us, with a note telling me not to wait up and to sleep in my room tonight, which meant that I had disgusted him to the point that he could not stomach my company.

Sadness washed over me. I would do better next time. I would make him proud. I had to. I just needed to figure out how.

The next day, there was another note telling me that he would be gone for a few days, and that I needed to stay inside. I didn't like to disobey, but I did like to push the limits. I was not going to stay inside for days. That was boring as hell. I walked through the woods to check the traps. Mercy was true to her word and was sitting by the tree that she had hid behind the day before, smiling like a Cheshire cat.

"You came." She said excitedly.

"Are you always this hyper?" I asked bemusedly.

"I'm just happy to have someone to talk to," she replied.

I didn't venture far, wanting to stay close so that if I heard Luke pulling up, I could run back inside before he saw me. He had ordered me to stay inside after all, but what he didn't know, would not hurt him or me. My skin was already carved with scars that someone else had earned for me, or thought that I had deserved.

"It looks like you didn't catch anything," she pointed out with a huge grin planted on her face as we approached the last trap.

I rolled my eyes and sighed. The lack of animals in my traps was putting me in a bad mood, but that it had somehow made her even chipper was downright pissing me off. Maybe Luke was right, I should have stayed home.

"It appears that way, huh?" I was aggravated, but I

couldn't really be mad at Mercy just because she didn't share in my misery. So I took a deep breath and fought the urge to grab her by the throat and snap her neck like the little rabbit that she resembled. "I'm going back in now. I guess I'll see you tomorrow?"

Her grin fell from her face. "Do you have to?" She scraped her toes against the ground, shy looking away.

"Yeah," I replied, "but I'll see you tomorrow, okay?"

"Deal."

"Alright, deal," I agreed. I didn't want to admit it, but I was actually looking forward to having her company when I walked through the woods.

---

I WAS GETTING USED to Mercy's visits, even looking forward to them. Just having human contact had kept me from going stir crazy.

She usually chattered about nonsense. She told me about her life as a runaway, and that she was squatting in a building on the other side of the woods. She was always fascinated by my hunting technique but only as a spectator, she said that it would hurt her heart if she had to do it herself. She didn't think that she would be able to bring herself to kill an animal.

Oddly, her innocence made me start to care about her, and so I took her under my wing. Our meet-ups in the woods became a regular thing, something that we both looked forward to. She began asking me to take her to my house. She was very curious about my place. The more that I said no, the more persistent she had become. When she asked why she could not come to my house, I lied and said that my daddy was extremely ill, and that he didn't want visitors. I also told her that was why, if there was ever a day that I didn't show up, it was because he needed me to take care of him, and I would have to meet her the next day. She told me that she understood, even if she did look a little sad. Honestly, I think that she was just relieved to have somewhere to go most days.

Whenever it started to get dark, I would always part ways with her, so that I knew that she would make it home safe. I had given her a pocket knife to carry for protection and had taught her the best spots to stab an attacker if she ever found herself in that unfortunate situation.

There came the day that she met up with me. There were bruises all over her face, and she was walking with a limp. I looked her up and down, trying to stop my heart from beating so fast, when the girl burst into tears and threw her arms around me.

Not sure how to handle this, I hesitantly wrapped my arms around her and tried my best to calm her down.

"Mercy, tell me what happened. Who did this to you?" I tried and failed miserably not to sound angry. I wanted to gut someone for hurting my friend. Someone had to pay.

"T-this guy," she started in a shaky voice, "he is a new squatter. He f-forced himself on me, and when I t-tried to get away, h-he hit me." She was crying nonstop. "Eve I was a v-virgin. He took that away f-from me." She fell to the ground sobbing. My heart broke for her. I remembered when Luke had taken my virginity and the pain it incurred. I was tough, but Mercy was not.

How dare this asshole take advantage of this sweet young girl? "Mercy, take me there."

She looked up from the ground, shaking her head as if to say no with a petrified expression on her face. She inhaled sharply and then exhaled slowly, trying to steady her nerves. "Please don't make me go back there. I cannot. He is there. I snuck out. He told me that he owns me now."

I gave her my blankest stare. Predators show no

emotions. That was my lessons kicking in. "Show me who he is." She hesitantly got up. We walked quietly through the woods. She took my hand and held on to it the entire way. She needed my support; I knew that. I needed to kill the bastard who hurt my friend. In some way, I think she knew that too.

We came out of the woods in a clearing behind an abandoned four-story building. "This is where I live," she whispered.

I nodded, not needing to say anything, just squeezing her hand in encouragement. I knew how hard that this must be for someone as fragile as she was.

"I want you to point him out to me," I instructed her, "then go back outside and wait for me."

She looked up at me, tears streaming all down her bruised face, and then she hugged me tightly. "Please be careful," she whispered in my ear. I nodded, holding back a predatory grin. She didn't need to worry about me, but it was nice that she did.

There were many people sleeping in the building. Most of them had set up their own permanent little residence with cots, coolers and even a blanket fort. It was interesting to know that childhood imagination was nothing more than preparation for homelessness.

Mercy pointed to a lump that was sleeping naked

in a huddled mess on the fourth floor. She started shaking. I saw the pelt of the rabbit that she had asked for and some other little items that we had found in the woods during our time together. This must be her room, and this guy decided that he would prey on the weakest one and steal everything about her, including her body.

Well, that was his first mistake. His second mistake was being brave enough to sleep after attacking a girl. I looked pointedly at the hallway so she would know to leave. She nodded solemnly and then hurried out, glancing back at me from the doorway. I smiled briefly at her so that she would go.

I walked over to the snoring man. His flaccid cock was stuck to his upper thigh, caked with her dried virginal blood. Fucking piece of shit. I took out my knife, kneeling down by the sleeping form. I shoved the sharp tip in where I would assume his spleen was. I wanted him to bleed. A lot. I pulled the knife out and stabbed him again. It felt good, pushing the blade inside his wet, warm body. I kept stabbing him, over and over, never letting the blade slide into the same hole twice. During the process, his eyes flew open from the pain hitting him. The shock of realization that a stranger was attacking him showed in his fearful eyes. He began to flail and tried to get up, until I straddled him, pinning his arms down to his body with my legs.

"You like to attack young girls?" I asked in a growl. "How do you like this?" I sneered at him as I bent down and clamped my teeth around the soft, pulsating flesh of his neck. I ripped my head back, taking out a bloody chunk. His mouth opened in a loud, squealing scream. I spit the chunk of flesh into the gaping hole. He gasped and gurgled as his own meat lodged in his throat. I placed my hands over his mouth and nose, letting him suffer as he slowly suffocated. He began twitching and jerking, his legs kicking, and his arms pushing against my thighs in a failed attempt at flailing. I kept eye contact as he choked to death on the chunk of his neck, his face turning from a bright, angry red to a deep shade of purple. Thick veins bulged in his face, and I smiled sweetly at him as his body went limp and the light left his wide, horrified eyes.

I stood up, covered in his blood, and gathered Mercy's stuff. Once I had everything, I walked out of the building and met Mercy. She took one horrified look at me and then threw up. I looked down at myself with a shrug. I guess I did look like I had just taken a bath in blood.

"Do you have someplace else where you can sleep?"

"Do I need to worry that he will find me?" She asked in a scratchy voice.

"No. He will not be bothering anyone anymore," I said dismissively, "but your room is trashed. You need to go somewhere else." I needed to get her settled somewhere so that I could go home and get cleaned up before Luke saw me in this state.

She gawked at me with a confused expression. I realized that she must be in shock. I sighed audibly. "Mercy. I need you to focus. You are safe, but I need to know that you have a place to stay now. I don't want to leave you here. You seriously don't want to go back to that room, trust me."

She nodded meekly and then looked at a building across the street. I took her hand and walked with her over to it. There was a water spicket on the side of the building. Bending low and turning it on, I cupped my hands and splashed the water on my face. The coolness was soothing. I stripped out of my outer shirt; it was completely soaked in blood. My undershirt was not as bad, but my jeans were just as done for as my outer shirt. I balled up my shirt. I could just pitch it in the fire when I got home along with my pants.

I looked at her with a soft gaze so as not to spook her more than she already was. When I caught her attention, I nodded toward the water and stepped away so she could rinse off and get a drink.

"Thank you." She quivered as she bent down to take a drink.

After she had her fill, I smiled down at her and took her hand, leading her into the building. I wanted to make sure that she had a safe place to sleep, without having to worry about a pervert taking advantage of her vulnerability. It was pretty beat up inside, fading and chipped paint and dirty floors, but we found an empty room that seemed somewhat habitable. Unlike the dregs that occupied the last building, this one seemed to house mostly families. I talked to some of the women, explaining what had happened to Mercy. They were outraged, telling me that they had kicked that same man out of their building the night before for harassing the women. This building had more men who could protect the women than the other place. It was definitely a step up, and I felt comfortable enough to leave her in their care.

Ready to go home, I told her that if she felt like she needed to rest for a few days, to do it. I would be around when she was ready. I had a $20 bill in my pocket. I pulled it out, shoved it in her hand and muttered, "For food." We hugged briefly, and then I left. This was one of the rare times I hoped that my brother was not there.

On my way home, I noticed a moving van in front of the house that was on this side of our lot. The secluded properties were not visible to the other due to the stretch of woods between them. I just happened to have walked past a small clearing in the copse of oak. I would have to snoop, to learn about the new neighbors, but it would need to wait until another day. Right now, I had to get home and make myself presentable.

## 5

## EVE

Luke was spending more and more time away. I slept in his bed at first in hope that he would wake me up when he came in, knowing that I was at risk of being punished, but I missed his touch. He would either not come home or would just sleep on the couch, instead of getting into bed with me.

One morning, I came into the kitchen and saw him drinking coffee while reading the paper. Joy filled my soul to see him there. It was becoming such a rare sight that I looked at him with a swell of hopefulness.

"Luke?"

He finished what he was reading before he acknowledged me. Then he pulled the paper down and lifted his eyebrows in response.

I was suddenly stricken with nervousness,

knowing that I was treading on thin ground. His somber expression told me as much. I asked, "Did I do something wrong?"

"I don't know. Did you?" He gave me an impartial shrug.

"I-I meant…" I was flustered for a moment, not sure how to respond.

"What do you mean, Eve?" He was becoming visibly irritated, which was only making me shake more.

"Y-you don't touch me anymore." I said, barely above a whisper.

As he stared at me, his expression hardened. I felt my stomach drop. I was not sure what was going on but I could tell that it was bad. His eyes narrowed and he said, "When I can trust you again, I will touch you. You have proven yourself unworthy."

My eyes welled with tears. I wanted to sink into the ground, knowing that he was disappointed with me. I didn't know what he meant by it, but if he was this angry with me, I must have let him down somehow. I heard his chair scoot back over the linoleum. The next thing I knew, he was grabbing my arm. Without a single word, he dragged me to the cellar.

I begged and pleaded for him not to do this. I told him that I would do better. He smirked at me maliciously, shoving me so hard inside the cellar that I hit the ground with a loud thud, the weight of my body landing on my arm. The door slammed shut as he locked me in darkness. I winced as I sat up, holding my elbow as the sting from the impact spread up and down my limb.

No matter how much older that I became, the cellar didn't get any less daunting. At least it was bigger than the closet that my mom used to keep me locked away. I wracked my brain, trying to figure out what my misdeed was. What was he talking about? Since I first came to live with Luke, I tested my boundaries with him, sure. But I thought that he admired my belligerence sometimes, even though it pissed him off when I disobeyed. Apparently, this was clearly one of those times.

I sat in the bleak blackness, surrounded by my thoughts. The realization of what it must have been that I had done wrong hit me as if it were a physical blow to my gut. In a panic, I began to pace. I yelped when I hit my elbow on the wall, trying to feel my way around in the dark. Mercy. He knew about Mercy. Shit. Now, because I became close to her, her life just became more dangerous than it had already been. He had always told me never to involve anyone else in our life. They would not understand our family, and family was all that was important.

Damn it, I was so stupid. This was all my fault. If I would have just listened to him, not been so stubborn, and stayed home… He had given me these rules for a reason; she would not be a part of our fucked up life. I would go see her one last time when and if he let me out of here, and then I will tell her that I was moving far away so she would not come around anymore. That should keep her safe.

Now, I needed to focus on getting in his good grace again. I would prove myself worthy. Shaking my head, I curled my lip, disgusted at myself for being such a terrible sister to him. He didn't ask much from me, I could have listened to him, but, instead, I always had to push him. I had to test the limits. As much as I needed his touch and his approval, I just could not seem to stop myself from being such a pain in his ass. I felt the urge to take a strip of skin from my leg and cursed that I didn't have a knife on hand. Needing to feel something, some sort of punishment, I slammed my face against the wall. Pain erupted in my nose, but it didn't bleed. I could not even do that right.

I slid down to the dirt floor, kicking the metal bucket along the way. That would be my bathroom as long as I was in here. I felt my chest tightening up. The panic was setting in. Taking deep breaths, I tried to stave off the attack. Nervously, I shoved my hand in my pocket, and I was rewarded with the hard bulge of my knife.

I laughed hysterically. It was there the whole fucking time.

I pulled it out, but my shaky hands fumbled and it fell to the floor. Feeling around for it, I felt something skitter across my hand. Normally, that would not bother me, but in the dark, it scared me, making me wrench my sore elbow.

I took a few deep breaths, trying to calm my nerves. Doing a half-assed job, I gave up and began feeling around for the knife again. After numerous swipes of my hand back and forth, extending my arm outward, I finally found it. I breathed a sigh of relief and grabbed it as if it were my lifesaver, flipping it open.

I looked down at where I knew my legs to be and pursed my lips. Changing my mind, I pulled up my shirt up. I felt the blade press into my side and then the blood drizzling down my waist. The endorphins that came with the pain of the cut finally brought me back from my ledge.

He would be pissed about that too, but I needed to be calm if I was going to be stuck in this dark hell. I could not let myself think of Mercy. I could not let myself think of everything wrong that I had ever done. I could not let myself think of anything else that was going to set off another panic attack. There was nothing that I could do to solve any of my issues while I was trapped in here.

Being in this situation, in the silence, blackness, oblivion, it always made me think of my childhood. There were things that I had locked away inside of my head that I did want not let out. This room didn't give me that option. As much as I tried to keep them shoved away, they continuously slammed into me as if they became physical manifestations. My mother had no problem with letting men use her body. However, sometimes those men wanted to include me. If it meant more drugs for her, she gladly let them add me to the mix.

Her only rule was no penetration. Apparently, in her addled brain, that was her being mother of the year. She would chain me by my ankle to the leg of the coffee table, and whatever the men wanted, I was expected to participate. The chain ensured that I didn't run away. It ranged from me just watching, because that was what got some of them off, to me suckling my mom's breasts like a baby while they fucked her, to me fondling their balls while they were inside my mother. She always made me strip down for the men. I was disgusted and humiliated but I knew the beating I would get if I refused.

One man in particular always made me press my

lips to her pussy while he jerked off and came all over her face. He would hold the back of my head, pushing my face so tightly against her that it was difficult to breathe. He was a weekly visitor, and every third or forth visit, he would pull his dripping cock away from her face, yank on my hair until I was staring up at him, and he would rub his come-coated cockhead across my lips. I hated that the most. Somehow, no matter how tightly I clamped my mouth shut, the salty, poignant taste would stay on my tongue for the rest of the night. When I complained about it, my mom would blacken my eye and throw me back into the closet.

The last time that he came around, he had tried to stick his cock in my mouth, and then, when I bit him, he slapped me so hard that he knocked me unconscious. I didn't mean to bite him, but my mouth was just too small. Thankfully my mom took that off the table from there on out. I guess she was the only one allowed to knock me around.

Sitting in here brought back every depraved act that I had suffered at the hands of my mother. I could remember each of their faces, each act, how gross I felt, how my mother would moan and writhe. I never let anyone else know about these memories. Not even Luke. It didn't matter since she was already dead.

Eventually, I dozed off. I was not sure for how long, but a scraping sound startled me awake. I could not see anything, but I knew it was something inside the metal bucket. I hated not being able to see what I was sticking my hand inside. If I dumped the bucket, whatever was in there could run out and bite me. I would rather grab it and kill it. The problem was that if I reached into the bucket, and it has its mouth open, because of course, I expect it to be a rat with ten-inch teeth, well, here goes to losing a hand.

I swallowed my trepidation and reached in, quickly running my hand around to find the culprit. Once I had my hand around it, I chuckled as I squeezed it and heard the shell crack as something gooey squished through my fingers. It was a beetle or some kind of hard-shelled bug. Well now, at least I could take a piss without it biting my ass.

My stomach growled, and its rumbling was loud. I thought about the bug carcass, but decided that I was not there yet. Who knew for how long I would be in here. I needed to try to focus my thoughts today, if it was day, on how to make it better with Luke. As much as the thought of giving up my friendship with Mercy hurt me, he would always be my first priority. It really was too bad. I think if he would get to know her, he would like her. She had the kind of personality that you could not help but be attracted to and feel an urge to protect.

Although, I suppose if she did meet him, and he did form a bond with her, he may prefer her to me. That would break my heart on so many levels.

I tried to do exercises to make the time go by, but with the lack of food and water, my body was worn out. I used the bucket one last time, thankful that I always wore two shirts so that I could use one to wipe, and then laid my head down to go back to sleep.

I woke up with a fierce hunger. I stood up and became dizzy. Was he ever going to let me out or was I going to die in here? I could not tell how long I had even been in here. And I had to wonder if he even planned to let me out. I guess if it was time for me to go, I was ok with it. I mean, I was not suicidal, but if I happened to die, it would not be a tragedy. I just wished that I could do it with food in my belly. For some reason that made me giggle to myself.

Then the thought occurred to me, spiraling around my mind in a maddening arc. I had plenty of food. My body was covered in meat. It was not as if I had issues with cutting myself, and it was not as if I had issue with eating raw meat. I did it all the time with the animals that I found in the woods. I felt around for my knife. I could not see, so I had to do this by memory.

I found it.

I picked it up and placed the blade against my arm, took a deep breath, and then pointed the tip down and sliced across until a strip of skin was hanging off. Carefully, by touching the end of the strip, I cut it off. The endorphins ran through me, but I was too weak to enjoy it. I hoped that it would not bleed too much. I could already feel blood streaming down my arm.

I tentatively touched the meat to my lips. As I started to put it in my mouth, my eyes glazed over. With barely a taste of my flesh on my tongue, I felt myself sliding down to the ground.

Then darkness swallowed me whole.

6

MERCY

When Eve left, I was not sure if I was more scared of her or the idea of being alone and defenseless again. In my mind, all I could think of was that she was a total badass, but in reality, she was a cold-blooded killer.

I could not be mad at her. She did just defend me and probably saved my life. He would have made my life miserable; there was no doubt about it. I also think that I have seen him pimp girls out before. Sleep was not going to come to me tonight, or any night soon. So I thought, until I dozed off. I woke up as someone dropped a warm blanket over me. Startled, I backed away from the older woman who was covering me up with a concerned look on her face.

"It's alright. I just wanted to check on you." She

spoke softly. "I told your friend that I would keep an eye on you." Smiling kindly, she reminded me of what a normal grandmother must look like. Not that I knew what normal was. She shuffled out of the room as I snuggled up into the blanket. My nether region was sore and achy. What if he had gotten me pregnant? What if I got some kind of STD? What if this was always going to be my existence, and I was never going to have a conventional sex life now that he had desecrated me? So many questions overloaded my mind, but no answers accompanied them.

The sun was shining in the window of my room when I woke up the next morning. Thankfully, Eve had grabbed my bag and belongings from the other building, so I didn't need to go out today at all. I had water and some cereal bars that she had given me. Hopefully, she wouldn't worry about me, I just didn't have it in me to leave the confines of this safe place, and to be honest, I didn't have it in me to face her today. I loved her for taking care of the threat, but the fact remained that she scared the ever-living fuck out of me.

I slept most of the day away, and my body seemed to crave the rest. Utter exhaustion took me over clear into the next day. I was stiff when I finally stood up but thankful that I hadn't been bothered. I stepped outside to a dreary sky. It was overcast, and there were storm clouds on the horizon. Taking a deep breath, I smiled, loving the smell of this kind of weather. Storms always fascinated me. The electricity, the power, the sensation of being swept away. I knew most people thought I loved a dreary life, but I was thankful each morning that I woke up and had survived another day. I never took life for granted.

I wanted to go see Eve. I felt guilty that I hadn't properly thanked her. She must have thought that I was angry with her, having stayed away for the day. She was truly the only friend I had ever had. She knew everything about me, admittedly, but I knew next to nothing about her home life. That was all right, I guess. She was not comfortable sharing about her family. I could understand that.

It was quiet when I walked to our spot in the woods, until the first raindrops started to fall. It was like the soft beating of a drum, tapping on the leaves. Smiling, I sat down on a log, and waited. She never showed. I would try again tomorrow.

And the next day, and the next day, but she never showed.

Something was wrong. I knew the rule; I was never to go to her place. Her daddy was very ill, and it made him very angry to have anyone there. I got it.

I would not like having strangers gawk at me when I was ill either. I didn't want to get her in trouble, but I was worried about her. I made my way through the woods to the outermost edge. Not exactly sure which house was hers, the one on the farthest left had a minivan with a lot of baby equipment in the open garage. The one on the far right looked abandoned. My guess would be the one on the right. It was foreboding. Just like Eve.

Timidly, I walked over, seeing a car in the driveway, and knocked on the door. The person who answered the door was not what I expected. He was a young man, very handsome, and yet had an air of darkness about him. Even when he smiled, it just felt wrong.

"May I help you?" he drawled.

"Hi." I was stumped and trying to come up with something quick. "My name is Mercy. I am a friend of Eve's. I just wanted to check on her." I stood there looking stupid as I gawked at him, trying to hide the fact that I was shaking.

"Mercy," he repeated, his brows furrowing. "Eve has told me a lot about you." His words flowed smoothly, like molasses pouring over bread. "Please come in while I get her."

Oh, well, ok, if she had told him about me, then it must be ok. She had never mentioned tall, dark, and dangerously yummy to me, but I planned to drill her on that later.

Smiling, still slightly unsure, I stepped inside. He pointed to a chair at the table, handed me a cup of tea, and walked into another room.

Happy to sit down, and realizing how intensely thirsty I was, I drank half the cup of tea in one swallow. I chuckled to myself. Oh, good going, Mercy, it's probably poisonous tea, just as my eyes started to swim and my head hit the table.

7

EVE

Waking up on a floor was never a pleasant experience. Especially when you were covered in your own blood and urine. Apparently, when I passed out, my bladder decided it wanted to let loose. Good times were had by all. Shaking my head, I squinted at the bright light. Wait. Bright light? The door was open. There was a bottle of water beside me. I took the cap off and then opened my mouth. I tilted the bottle up, draining half of its contents because my throat was a baked wasteland.

I sat up slowly to make sure I stayed steady, and then I put my hands on the cold, stone wall to brace myself as I stood up. My knees were shaky, but so far so good. Slowly, I walked out of the cellar and into the blinding light.

I stood there until my eyes adjusted. I didn't hear

any sounds. I could not decide if I needed to eat or get myself cleaned up first. My arm looked really bad, maybe even infected, but I was starving. I decided to go to the kitchen. There was a note on the table.

*Do not leave this house. Get cleaned up, and I will be home for supper. We have a special guest joining us. Tonight we are having a BBQ in your honor, so I can remind you how special you are to me.*

*Love, Luke*

HE SAID I was special to him. I was not sure about the special guest thing, but who the fuck cared? Luke still wanted me and loved me. I was so happy that I almost fell. A wave of dizziness washed over me. I steadied myself and then went to the refrigerator. I pulled out the grape jelly. The peanut butter was in the cupboard, beckoning me. My belly rumbled in anticipation. I slapped some of both on two pieces of bread and wolfed it down. The cold jelly felt so good on my throat. It was just what I needed. It also gave me enough energy to get myself cleaned up and put on something special for him tonight.

Taking a shower was painful, the water sliced through all the cuts and abrasions. My arm was definitely infected. There was green pus coming from it. I would need to put some antibiotic ointment on it. In the meantime, I would wear a long sleeved shirt so as not to anger Luke.

In the next few days, I needed to find Mercy, and end all ties with her so that she would be safe. I had money saved away. I would give her a chunk of cash so she could start over fresh somewhere else. She deserved that. She was a good kid who just happened to have been dealt a shit hand in life.

8

MERCY

WAKING up in a cage was the worst feeling that I supposed anyone could ever feel. Since this was not my first time being in one, it ranked right up there for me. I was actually sitting there wondering if the rape was worse than being trapped in this cage. Sadly, the rape was not as traumatic.

When my eyes opened, and I realized what I was inside of, and who probably put me here, since he was the last person I had seen, I tried to scream. That was when the realization hit me like a smack in the face that my mouth was taped shut with duct tape. But not just that. Tape I could probably wiggle my lips around and get out of, there was something more. I tried to open my mouth, without avail, but was able to open my teeth a little, ran my tongue outside. Some kind of wire. A thick wire stuck to the tape. Holy fuck. He sewed my mouth shut. How long was I out?

The cage was small; my knees were up around my bowed head. I tried to wriggle my hands free from under me, thinking that the weight of my body kept them trapped, and that the constraints of the cage kept me from freeing them. It was worse than that, though. He had tied my wrists with chicken wire to the bottom of the cage, and that was the reason why I could not move them.

This was why I had become a runaway. My mother and father had kept me in a cage because they never wanted children and could not be bothered to take care of one. They would throw dog food in the cage for me to eat. I would have to drink from a hose that they slipped through each night, which was what they also had used to clean me. The water had been ice-cold, but it was the only way to get the urine and feces off me until I mastered how to go without getting it all over myself in the cage. When I was eleven years old, I had finally broken free, running as far as I could, as fast as I could, I and never looked back. I learned how to live on the streets. Now, six years later, I was back in a fucking cage.

I didn't know who this psychopath was, or how he knew that this was my biggest fear, but when Eve found me here, she would set me free. I had faith in that.

My heart was constricting. I didn't know if it was day or night. There was a cover or some type of tarp thrown over the cage. I felt as if I were suffocating as the tears streamed down my face, desperately choking down every gasp of moist air that I could. I swore to myself that I would not let him break me, but a part of me wondered if it was too late. I could feel my nose running all over my face. That was my pet peeve. Funny, out of all the shit happening, that was what I focused on, but my mind was a danger zone right now and if I didn't focus on something so mundane, I felt like I may check out for good.

I decided to pray for the first time in years. Maybe this was my penance for not keeping up on it. I prayed the night that I got away and thanked God with all my heart for letting me get away safely. I swore that I would never ask for anything or do anything wrong. And I had not. I had never stolen a thing, done anything immoral, lied or cheated. I would go without first.

Now, here I was, praying with all my might, begging him to save me from this place of torment. You had to be tough when you lived on the street. I kept up that façade until the assault. This was like a ripple effect. He started my ruination and this was ending it. Was this all that my life was going to amount to, really? She was not going to come rescue me. If she were, she would have already been here.

My hope was demolished. This man, whose name I didn't even know, had broken me.

## 9

## EVE

Have you ever had one of those clarifying moments in your life? You know the type, where you knew that you were being taught a lesson, but your mind rebelled against it. The one thing that I had been taught since coming to live here was that family always came first. That shit could be tattooed all over my body. I would tell you that without hesitation. Who was my family? Luke was. He was my family. The one person who would always come first no matter what. But, sometimes, that was a bitch of a pill to swallow.

Luke came home very happy. He was smiling from ear to ear, asking me how I was feeling, telling me if the cookout went well. He told me that I would end up in his room tonight and not the cellar. I didn't want to be back in that fucking cellar. No matter what happened tonight, I would make sure he was satisfied.

"Can I help you?" My eyes lit up hopefully. I wanted to show him that I had learned my lesson.

"Not yet, Eve. Do you remember the forbidden fruit?"

I furrowed my brow vaguely remembering that reference. "Ummm, yes."

"Tonight we will see if you will eat from it." His smile didn't quite reach his eyes.

Not knowing exactly what he meant, I said, "I will do whatever you wish me to do. I want you to see how sorry I am that I disappointed you." I lowered my eyes to the ground submissively.

He grunted, turning away. Pouring myself a cup of tea, I sat at the table to wait for him to tell me what he wanted from me. I also wondered what time our guest would show up. Surprised that he would even invite anyone; he was always so adamant about not having anyone come to our home.

He handed me carrots, lettuce, and tomatoes to cut. So I had salad duty. I could handle that. I started humming while I was chopping. I looked up to see him staring at me. He was smiling, so I smiled back. He said, "You look nice, Eve. Thank you."

Moisture filled my eyes. It had been so long since he complimented me. "I love you, Luke."

He nodded his head, still smiling. Then he turned and walked out the door. Smiling broader now, I finished chopping the salad with more enthusiasm, drank my tea, and waited for more instructions.

He was building a fire pit when I peered out the window. I wish he would let me help, but I supposed that because I was in this dress, he didn't want it ruined. I loved the way his muscles rippled. Those strong arms had aroused me and abused me so many times, and I could not wait for the next one hundred thousand times. I didn't care if it was beating or fucking, I just needed to feel his touch. He unknowingly kept me grounded. I would probably be dead right now, or worse, a junkie, if it were not for him kidnapping me.

He turned around to see me staring; I swear the man had a sixth sense. He winked, and I blushed. You would think after all this time he would not have that effect, but he did.

I decided that I better relieve myself in the bathroom and check my arm so it didn't bleed out on my dress. Putting a clean bandage on, peeing, and then brushing my hair one last time, I walked into the kitchen as he was calling for me, beckoning me to come out. I looked at the table for the salad but it was gone. He must have already came and got it.

I walked outside with a huge smile stretched

across my face, shielding my eyes from the sun. I looked up at the pyre he built, and then stopped dead in my tracks. Horror washed over me. My mouth dropped open as I saw Mercy tied to the wood like a sacrifice. "W-what? I don't understand," I stammered.

"Oh, I see you noticed our guest."

"Luke, please." I saw the fear on her face. She was awake but not making a sound. The closer that I got, I saw what he had done. He had sewn her lips together. The skin around her mouth was bleeding as if tape had been ripped off. Feeling the bile rise in my throat, I looked at him, pleading with my eyes.

"You have to make a choice. Family or this wretch." He picked up a torch and then lit it before holding it out toward me.

He wanted me to burn Mercy at the stake. How on Earth was I supposed to do that? Why could he not just have killed her? It still would have hurt, but not like this.

"Just do it." I said numbly.

"No. You have to choose. Vocally. If you choose her, you untie her, and then you can both go away free. But you can never return. If you choose family, then you burn her, the one you disobeyed me with, you show me you have learned your lesson, and all is forgiven, our night goes forward as you would like." His expression hardened.

Sadness washed over me. There was no choice. I could not do this to someone that I loved. I could not betray them. Love is such a fickle thing. I shook my head, clenching my jaw. I stepped away from Luke, who sighed deeply as he still held his torch. I walked over to Mercy, whose eyes had relief in them. My smile hardened.

"My sweet friend, death is so beautiful. It liberates you, sets you free." The tears were streaming down my face. "There is nothing I would rather share with you than your last minutes on Earth." Mercy's face was frantic as she realized that the reprieve that she thought I would offer her would not be coming. "You see," I continued, "there is no choice for me. Family will always come first."

I pulled a candle lighter out of my pocket and lit the bottom of her pants. The smell of the lighter fluid that he had poured all over her permeated my senses. It didn't take long for the wood to engulf in flames and quickly spread up her body. Her mouth tore open, her lips ripping to shreds as they pulled away from the wire, and her high-pitched scream pierced the sky. She wriggled frantically, futilely trying to escape. Black smoke covered her anguished, pain-filled face.

Luke's laugh, as well as his arms wrapping around my stomach, telling me how proud he was of me, finally shook me out of my trance. I was disgusted with the situation, knowing that if he had given me the choice, I would have traded places with her. I did this to her. I knew it, and he knew it. He knew that I knew it. He was going to make sure that I never forgot the rules again.

"Ready to eat?" He smiled at me. "You had me worried there for a moment." The disturbed look on my face made him chuckle.

We sat down at a picnic table, ate salad, hot dogs and baked beans while he made me watch the fire burn every inch of her. My heart was broken. I could not show it, but I certainly could not be upbeat and happy.

When the sun went down, he doused the fire with a hose. He took my hand and led me inside the house. I knew as soon as I had alone time, I would grieve the loss of Mercy and my part in it all. I would never forget the look of betrayal on her face. Before this, I would have never felt guilty about any life that I had taken. Now, I could hardly breathe from the weight of the guilt. It was stronger than gravity in its weighing me down, pushing me to the earth.

Luke was so pleased with my decision; he was still holding my hand. "So I made a decision to help you stay at home. You need something more to do to keep you occupied."

Looking at him, I waited for what new task I would have. He began to undress. Then he sized me up, and a corner of his mouth lifted. He tilted his head, waiting for me to disrobe. I hurriedly took everything off, and then I saw him frowning at the bandage on my arm.

"What do you want me to do?" I asked as he pushed me on the bed.

"You don't know what to do?"

"No. I mean, yes," I stammered. "Here, I know what to do. I meant to keep me occupied."

He waggled his eyebrows. "Well, I usually wear a condom when I do this, but I think it's time that we become a real family. You are going to have my baby." He slammed his cock into me before I could register what he had just said. As he was rutting on top of me hard and fast, I was in shock. There was no damn way. I didn't want to be a mother. I was too young. I didn't even like kids. His hand was around my throat, squeezing tighter and tighter as he came closer and closer to release, I was gasping for air when he finally emptied all of his load inside of me, burying his cock deep to ensure that it took.

All I could think of was how much I wanted to get to the bathroom and try to get every last drop of his come out of me. He was not having it. He told me that I had to lie at the end of the bed with my legs up, so that the sperm could take hold. I was shaking so hard, which he assumed was because he fucked me so hard. In no way was I having a fucking kid. No way.

10

EVE

Luke didn't stay home for long. He was more restless than I was. He did keep us in money and food, so I understood that he could not be there all the time. He was always checking to see if I missed a period yet. Thankfully, I had not. He always looked so disappointed when I told him that; and this was the one time that I was ok with disappointing him. When he was home, it was the same routine; he would fuck me and then send me to my room.

He started being away more and more. He said that he would know if I left, so I had better stay inside. I asked if I could walk in the woods once a day. His immediate answer was no, but then he cocked his head, mulling it over. He finally relented but only as long as I didn't talk to anyone. The burnt pyre was left in the backyard as a reminder to me what happened when I disobeyed.

One day, I detoured from my usual route through the woods. I had been curious about the neighbors for a while now. I walked over to their house and peeked into their bedroom window. She was lying naked on the bed. He had his face buried in between her legs, and she had one hand holding his head down, while the other hand grasped the sheet behind her. I could hear her moans of ecstasy. She was writhing and bouncing all over the bed. Then she let out a loud screech, lifting her hips off the bed. He lifted up his head, covered in her juices. He slapped her leg, and then got on his knees.

She turned over, put her face on the mattress and her ass up in the air while he positioned himself behind her. It was so erotic, the way they moved together, the way they moaned in rhythm. It was almost as if they were one being. Luke and I were never like that. I didn't understand this kind of intimacy. It was making my stomach do flip-flops. He entered her from behind, pounding into her, driving deep inside. I was turning to leave when his eyes swung to me. Our eyes locked, and he watched me watch him as he continued fucking her without abandon. She was writhing underneath him, but he never lost eye contact with me. I think having me there drove him to fuck her even harder, thrusting deeper. He was getting off on my voyeurism. I had to admit that I was getting worked up as well. The lust on his face was making my pussy throb something fierce. When he was ready to release, he could not help but lose eye contact with me. I took the brief moment of opportunity to sneak away, flushed and out of sorts.

For the next couple of days, I made myself stay away from the house. It was abnormal to watch them. It was even worse to have it consume my mind so completely. I had been having dreams that I was lying under him, writhing as he drove himself inside me, filling me.

That was bad. I should only be dreaming about Luke. He was the only one who should be turning me on. Unfortunately, Luke didn't care if I was aroused or not. It only mattered to him that I took care of his needs. That I was readily available when he wanted me to be. I needed to focus on his needs and quit thinking of myself.

Three days later, I found myself bored again, so I thought that I would peek again. It was around the same time of day as the last time I found myself peering through their window. I knew that the chance of catching them in the throes of passion was minimal, but sure enough, they were going at it again. I was not sure whether or not they adhered to a strict lovemaking schedule, or if they just fucked like rabbits. And when I looked through the window, his eyes immediately swung over to me. Once again, our eyes locked. His were a piercing blue that almost mesmerized me. His dark raven-colored hair was wavy and accented his chiseled face. He smirked when he saw me. He never took his eyes off me.

For the next five days, we followed the same routine. They must have had a scheduled sex time, or he was purposely choosing that time in the hope that I would keep showing up. He really did seem to love having my presence there, my eyes roaming his body. There was a multitude of children's toys strewn about the room, littering the floor and stacked high on their dresser, and I had to wonder where they stashed their offspring when they were humping like horny, little bunnies. I had never seen a child. I only ever saw the two of them. And I was fine with that. I only came by for the free show, to feel something that was still foreign to me. Passion. Each time he finished, I would sneak away.

The next time that I came by, he was spanking her. She had her head tilted back; her mouth stretched open, strangled cries of ecstasy filling the room as his hand crashed repeatedly on her red, swollen ass cheeks. She was already coming all over his hand. He didn't even need to penetrate her in order to make her climax. Watching her ass ripple, his hand making those red marks all over her backside, from each impact was making me wet. He bent down and kissed each mark, and she mewled like a cat in response. Then he thrust two fingers inside of her as he swiped his tongue up and down the crack of her ass. I sucked in a breath that I didn't even realize that I was holding. I had never seen this done before. I honestly didn't know that this was even a thing. My mind whirled around the possibilities, and I imagined what it would feel like to be on my hands and knees with him behind me, his fingers searching my depths, his tongue twirling and sliding over my ass.

She was shoving her ass back into his face as he tongue-fucked her. Before I realized what I was doing, my hand was inside my pants, my fingers inside my wet pussy. He lifted himself up, replacing his fingers with his hard cock. That was when he saw me. He blew me a kiss and locked eyes with me as I furiously rubbed myself to orgasm. I didn't have a lot of experience with this but I knew that this felt fucking amazing. My eyes widened as the heights of pleasure consumed me. I squeezed my eyes shut until I came back down from the high. When I opened them back up, he was still staring at me, not having finished yet. I had to admit that knowing he was watching me come was so thrilling that I wanted to do it again and again. I now understood why he enjoyed having me spy on him so much. As soon as he saw me watching again, he finished inside of her. I wanted to run away, but my legs were rubbery. Instead, all I could do was slide down on to the ground.

I was not sure how long that I was out there. A minute? An hour? Eventually, he walked outside, and his face lit up when he saw me. "Hello, beauty. I was hoping that we would meet properly."

I needed to leave. I could not talk to him. I was embarrassed and humiliated. He had witnessed me have an orgasm. What had originally been a huge turn on was now turning my insides into mush.

"Don't be embarrassed," he said softly. When I responded with a shocked expression, he continued, "Your face is turning red."

"I'm sorry that I spied on you," I whispered.

"I'm not. You are sexy as hell. It is super hot knowing you are watching. It would be hotter if you would let me involve you."

I looked at him, feeling stricken. Did he just ask me to have sex with him?

"Isn't that your wife?"

"My girlfriend. She is taking the baby to her

mom's tonight for a couple of days if you want to come over tomorrow." He smiled encouragingly.

"N-no. I couldn't." I really could not. I didn't know the first thing about sex, besides the little that Luke had taught me. Plus, I needed to take care of a problem I had. I didn't need to involve anyone else in my life. This had to be my last visit.

He shrugged. "Up to you, beauty. I would love to taste every inch of you."

Those words crashed right through me, making my pussy throb. I needed to leave, and I needed to leave right now. So I jumped up and ran away.

11

JERRY

THERE SHE WAS AGAIN, watching us. This girl was so fucking hot. I needed to get a piece of her. I was not sure where she had come from; must be the other house, or maybe the other side of the woods. That other house looked abandoned.

Rena was taking Tyler to her mom's house. This would be the perfect time to get the peeping little vixen in bed. I thought that I had died and gone to heaven when I saw her arm shaking from her masturbating right outside the window, then her look of pure ecstasy when she reached her peak. Damn, it was the sweetest thing that I had seen in a long time. I was not even sure how old she was, but if she could come like that, I would have to take my chances.

So she liked me licking Rena's ass. I could do that

and so much more to her. She would be begging for more when I got a hold of that delectable body.

She seemed skittish when I talked to her, if I were a betting man though, she would show up, just out of curiosity, if nothing else.

12

EVE

HUMANITY WAS something not everyone was born with. I believed that mine had been beaten out of me. Luke, well, I believe he never had it to begin with. So the moral question here was, should either one of us procreate?

Maybe he, at some point, with the right woman, should. As much as that thought hurt me, him being with another woman, touching her, possibly tasting her, now that I knew that could be done, hurt me to my very core. I guessed that the reason why he didn't do these extra things with me was my ineptitude. And it was this inexperience that made the thought of him being with someone hurt so badly. Hell, I still could not even mother his child. There was not one maternal cell in my body. My mother was my role model. Really? I would do anything for Luke. Hell, I burnt my only friend to a crisp, but I would not birth a child. I just would not. I could not.

I needed to let some aggression out. I never did let my grief out for Mercy. And now, I think that I gave the guy at the other house the wrong impression. He thought because I watched him, I developed feelings of some kind for him. I would never cheat on Luke, and the fact that he would cheat on his girlfriend pissed me off. I would teach him a lesson tomorrow. Luke was coming home tonight to do his weekly pregnancy check.

I had lied to him last week, telling him I that hadn't missed my period. He seemed so deflated. He said that we would try again next week. So tonight, he would mount me again in hope of knocking me up.

I had dinner waiting for him when he came home. He looked exhausted as he ate the food, chewing dejectedly. When he finished, he pointed to the bedroom.

I could tell that he was not in a good mood, so I didn't try to engage him in conversation. I just undressed and bent over the bed. He came in from behind, entering me without preamble. Thrusting in and out until he finally grunted, pulled out and then told me to lie on his bed until morning. He walked out of the room, and a moment later, I heard the door open, the car start, and then drive away.

I didn't move because, at this point, it simply didn't matter. I knew that I was already pregnant. I saw a note on the table that he would be home in five days. I decided that I wanted to be creative with the guy next door, so I packed a bag. This would take more than my knife to prove my point about trying to take advantage of young girls.

I went over to his house and knocked on the door. He answered with a big smile on his face. He stepped back so that I could come inside. The house had many baby things in it. He saw me looking at all the things. "We have a nine month old," he explained.

I nodded.

He led me to the bedroom, trying to kiss me. I shied away. "I need to go slow."

He nodded his understanding, but the glare that crossed his face gave him away.

"As you can imagine, I am naïve about these things. I was hoping you would allow me to play."

He looked intrigued by that idea. "Tell me what you have in mind," he said smoothly.

"Well," I started, "would you be willing to wear a blindfold and let me use scarves to tie your hands around the chair handles?" I nodded my head toward the office chair at the desk in the corner of the room.

He was amused. I could tell by the crinkle of his eyes. "Then what?" he asked.

I acted nervous and shy. "Then, if it's ok, I would like to taste you." Smiling, I looked demurely at the ground.

His expression was of pure astonishment. "Absolutely, my beauty."

He undressed and then sat down, making sure he extended his legs so that his dick was sticking straight out at me. My eyes widened as I took him in. He was preening like a peacock.

I gulped as I pulled the scarves out of my bag. He could not stop smiling at the thought of my lips wrapped around him. I wrapped one scarf around his left wrist, pulling it tight to the handle so that his hand was flat against the wood grain. "Is that too tight?" I asked in a concerned voice.

He shook his head no, looking even more amused.

I nodded, and did the other wrist.

He asked if I would undress before I blindfolded him. I told him that I would take my shirt off for him, but if it were okay, the rest would come off when he took care of me after I played. He loved that idea.

I placed the scarf around his eyes, tying it snug around his head. A shiver went through his whole body. "You alright?" I asked.

"Just excited," he murmured in response. I glanced down at the pre-come on the tip of his penis and saw yes, indeed, that he was excited. "I wish I could watch." It came out in a kind of whine.

"Let me get started," I explained, "then I will take the blindfold off."

His breathing evened out until I ran my fingernails across his length. Then a small moan escaped his lips. I reached into my bag for the cordless nail gun. Now the real fun would begin.

I pushed the gun into him and pulled the trigger. The nail went through his hand. His shock registered as I was moving the gun to his other hand. A loud wail of pain pierced the silence as I nailed the other hand down. He was flailing and making a ruckus. I needed him to calm his kicking legs down before he connected with my face. His chair was on wheels but I still had the upper hand. He was blindfolded and in immense agony.

I pulled out my knife, came up behind him, grabbed one leg and sliced the tendon behind his ankle rendering his leg useless. I made quick work of doing the same to the other leg. It was easier than it should have been, but I did have the element of surprise on my side.

## 13

## JERRY

WHAT THE FUCK was this crazy bitch doing? She must have had me confused with someone else. I didn't do anything to deserve this. I could not even form a sentence; the pain was so fucking immense.

She finally took the scarf off my eyes. She was actually grinning. She was standing there looking happy. The crazy bitch! "Why?" I manage to grit out through my clenched teeth.

"Why? Because you are a piece of shit. A piece of shit who thought that he could prey on a young girl. Now I'm going to make you suffer for it."

Disbelief swam through me. I just wanted to have fun, and show her some fun. This bitch was a straight psycho. Poor Tyler would be growing up without a dad. Except his whore of a mom, Rena, would probably replace me as soon as she could.

Ow, fucking ow.

She was pressing on the nails in my hand. My eyes were streaming in tears, while my mouth was in a perpetual grimace of pain. I could not think a single coherent thought. In my mind, I was already doomed.

"Just kill me, and get it over with," I heard someone croak. Wait. Could that have been me saying that? Was I giving up?

"Anyone can die," she sneered. "It takes more courage to suffer. You have played your games, but you are playing my game now."

"How fucking insane are you?" I spat.

She arched her eyebrows and giggled. "Do I really need to answer that?"

Please let me die. Please let me die. I kept chanting to myself. That was when I heard the sound of a car door opening and shutting.

## 14

## EVE

COCKING MY HEAD, I saw the disbelief on his face when he realized his family was home. This was perfect. I could take care of them all. No fuss, no muss. Or maybe I explain about his cheating ass, and she can say sayonara. Shrugging, I walk out of the bedroom, leaving him whimpering, and wait for her to come into the house.

"Jerry? Hey, babe! We came home early because we missed you, Daddy." She sung out in a light voice, carrying a baby carrier. Still not noticing me standing there, she sat the baby down, turned around to look for him, and then settled her gaze on me. Her mouth formed an O shape.

"Oh, hello. Who are you?" She tried to sound nonchalant but failed.

"I'm Eve. Jerry is in the bedroom. Naked." A look

of disgust passed over her face. "He invited me over because you were gone," I said matter-of-factly.

She didn't have time to react before he yelled for her to run and that I was crazy. She looked at me and then at the baby. She grabbed her purse and tried to rummage in it, but she didn't quite make it before I reached her. I slammed into her, knocking her down. Grabbing her head, I slammed it on the floor multiple times. I didn't relent until she stopped moving.

She never had a chance to think. I felt that if she had had time to react, she would have been a worthy adversary. The baby started to get fussy. I curled my lip up, hating the sound of it. Spying a bottle in the seat, I shoved it in the child's mouth. Thankfully, it shut the kid up.

I bundled the blanket in the carrier and propped the bottle on it. Then I grabbed her purse to see what she was reaching for. Well, I hit the jackpot. She had a gun, which I aimed at her head and shot for good measure. I continued to rummage through her purse and found a taser. This, I could use to have fun with Jerry Boy. On further contemplation, the gun would be too quick for him. He didn't deserve a quick death.

I walked in, holding the gun in one hand and the taser in the other. He dropped his head and started weeping. His dick, oddly enough, was still standing at attention. I set my tools down and took out my knife. I grabbed his member with my free hand while he started chanting "no" in a low murmur, and cut it off. He didn't need it anymore.

He screamed, thrashing about, as blood spurted like a faulty fountain.

"Ssshhh," I cooed. "We're just getting started."

"What more can you do to me?"

"I killed my own mother. What do *you* think I could still do to you?" Laughing, I threw his now deflated penis on his bed.

"You are a fucking psychopath." His eyes began to roll into the back of his head.

I waited for the insult, but it never came. "Um, yeah? That is a given. Was there more to that thought, or was that just an observation?" He was starting to bore me. I used the taser on him. Wow, that little thing packed a lot of juice. I had to admit that watching him flail around was entertaining.

Until it became boring.

I decided that I needed to finish him off. I left, walking into the other room, to a wailing baby. I went over to look at him and stared down at him, wondering what to do. I pursed my lips. Maybe if I held him, he would quiet down. It might even make me feel differently about being a mother. I unbuckled him and pulled him out. He smiled and cooed up at me, grabbing my hair with his chunky little hands. I felt, well, I felt…

Absolutely nothing.

The baby's shirt was wet, so I removed it. I was not sure what made me do it, but I felt the need to see this child without a shirt. He was so plump and ticklish. He giggled when I ran my finger down his spine. I held him for a while, until he started to cry some more. I grabbed his bottle and took him in the room with his father. Laying him on the bed, I gave him the milk and focused on the slobbering mess in the chair that was Jerry.

As I walked to the bathroom, Jerry woke up. He yelled that the baby would fall off the bed. With everything going on, this was what he was worried about? I grabbed the supplies that I needed from under the sink.

When I walked back into the bedroom, I saw that he was indeed correct; the child was dangerously close to the edge. I scooped him up, and sat down with him on my lap.

"Thank you," he breathed out.

"Do you know how I skin animals?" I asked. He shook his head. His breathing was erratic.

I ran both of my thumbs in between the baby's

ribcage. "I sink my thumbs into the flesh right here and then pull. I don't need a knife, just my fingers."

He had a wary look on his face but kept quiet.

"What do you think, Jerry? Do you think I could skin a baby as easy as I can a rabbit?" I smiled sweetly at him.

His face dropped. He looked beaten. "Please, do whatever you want to me, just leave him alone."

"Fine. If you are giving me permission, open your mouth, drink this liquid Drano, and I will spare him." I shrugged.

His mortification was apparent, but he knew that it was either him or the baby.

He had no other choice, so he tilted his head back while opening his mouth. I put the little one on the floor and then picked up the liquid cleaner. I opened it, walked over to him, kissed him on the forehead and then poured the acid down his throat. I leaned in, brushing my lips against his ear and whispered, "I lied. I am skinning your boy."

I picked him back up and sat down with him on my lap. I needed to see if my theory was correct, if I could skin him without a knife. I pressed my thumbs just below his sternum and pushed as hard as I could, but his skin was tough. He began to scream, his deafening screeching grating on my nerves, so I eventually snapped his neck. I had to make two attempts. It seemed that babies were a little more durable than rabbits, but, eventually, the bones gave way.

My fingers were just not going to cut it, pun intended. If I used my knife, a small slit in the sternoclavicular area, I could peel the skin right off of him. So I went to work, slicing and peeling. Because this was new, fresh skin, it peeled like a banana, and the muscle was easier to dissect and filet off.

As I had done with so many little rabbits in the wood, I feasted. This truly was what I needed to purge my mind over Mercy. I decided to go home and clean up. I was full and exhausted.

## 15

### EVE

I SLEPT for almost two days straight. The adrenaline rush had worn me out. Now, I needed to decide what I was going to do about my problem. I knew from being around that baby that I didn't want to be tied down. I was not a mother. Luke would not understand if I skinned our child, and truly that was the only way I would have one. Well, maybe with a little barbeque sauce.

I went to my closet and took out a wire hanger. It may be crude, but it would do the trick. I unwound it so that it was straight. I went into the bathroom and then stripped down. I sat on the toilet, took the hanger and then slid it inside me. I pushed it in as far as it would go and then pumped it in and out, trying my best to scrape the inside. I was purely going on what I read. This had to work, and then I could do this every time until my uterus was too scarred to get pregnant. It didn't sound like a bad plan; the pain was exhilarating. I pulled the hanger out to see blood on it. I put it back in and started over to assure that it got it all. It was becoming painful as hell, but it was well worth it.

I needed to hide this hanger, so I put it in my closet, behind a loose board. My stomach cramped more and more as the day went on. When the cramps became mind numbing, I decided to lay down with a heating pad.

I dreamt about my mom that night. Everything seemed so surreal, like I was there, but I was not. I could feel myself shivering from the cold, but I was soaked in sweat. Someone was talking to me, but it was so far away. I could not quite hear them. I tried to pry my eyes open. They were so heavy, so I gave up and just let myself drift away.

Waking up was a bitch when there was someone chiseling away inside your head. I opened my eyes to see Luke sleeping by my bed. I was confused. Why was he asleep in a chair?

He opened his eyes as I sat up.

"I thought I might have lost you. Want to tell me what happened?" He rubbed his hand over the scruff on his face.

I looked perplexed because I really didn't know

what had happened. So I began to tell him about me killing the family next door. He never changed his expression, not until I came to the child.

He cleared his throat. "And this?" He held up the hanger.

Fuck, I was caught. "I can't be a mother. I am so sorry Luke. I wanted to do whatever it took to please you, but that is one thing I cannot do. I thought if I scarred my uterus enough, you would forget about it."

He nodded. "You thought it was ok to kill my baby?"

"What? No? I killed the neighbor's baby. He wasn't yours."

He held up the bloody tip of the hanger. Shit, I hadn't thought of it that way.

"Please forgive me. I'm so sorry." The paranoia in my voice made his head snap up.

"No, you aren't sorry yet. I walked in here to find you half dead from bleeding out because you killed my baby. You don't even know what sorry is. You want your uterus scarred? We will scar your uterus." He glared at me with cold, dead eyes.

He grabbed my legs and spread them apart. I didn't try to get away. I knew that I deserved whatever he did to me. I was sore already, so when he shoved his fist inside my pussy, the scream that I could not hold back, erupted like lava. My skin ripped as he pushed as far as he could with his entire arm inside of me. The look of determination on his face told me that this was not the end. I tried to bite my lip to keep myself from crying out, but the pain was excruciating. When he shoved his hand as far as he could inside of me, he spread his fingers and scraped his nails against the walls.

I almost passed out, except that when I teetered on the edge of blackness, he slapped my face to keep me awake.

"You are not worth my time anymore. I made a mistake in making you a part of my family." He spit in my face.

"No," I begged. "Please."

"You are nothing."

Those words tore me to shreds. He grabbed me by my hair and dragged me out in the yard. I thought that I was going to have the same fate as my friend, but then he uncovered a hole. It looked like some sort of well. He grabbed me by the neck and threw me over the edge.

The last visual I had of him was that night. He looked down the hole to see me sprawled on the ground looking up at him. The sun shown brightly behind his head like a fiery halo. He took his cock out and pissed down on me. I never saw him again.

I was not sure how many days had passed. My neck had broken when he threw me in, my body lying in a mangled heap. I would stay here until I withered and died.

My soul was already dead though, knowing that I let down the greatest man on Earth.

## THE END

THE INFERNO WORLD

DIVE INTO THE DARK, TABOO WORLD NOW!

Inferno by Yolanda Olson
BUY: http://myBook.to/Inferno_
Cinere by Yolanda Olson
BUY: http://myBook.to/CINERE
Sparks by Yolanda Olson
BUY: http://myBook.to/Sparks-

INFERNO WORLD NOVELLAS

Verboten by AA Davies
BUY: https://amzn.to/2Q7hw5f
TBR: http://bit.ly/GRVerboten

Malignus by Dani René
BUY: https://amzn.to/2LoPnYG
TBR: http://bit.ly/MalignusTBR

Iniquity by Emery LeeAnn
BUY: https://mybook.to/myIniquity
TBR: http://bit.ly/IniquityTBR_

Burned by Jennifer Bene
BUY: https://amzn.to/2YwdEO2
TBR: http://bit.ly/2DCHdp6

INFERNO WORLD NOVELLAS

Obloquy by Murphy Wallace
BUY: https://amzn.to/2YxmhIk
TBR: http://bit.ly/Obloquy

Embers by Yolanda Olson
An Inferno Conclusion
BUY: https://amzn.to/30pLJRG
TBR: http://bit.ly/2DAPVUO

OTHER BOOKS BY EMERY LEEANN:

Disturbed (free standalone short story)

http://myBook.to/getDisturbed

**The VooDoo Lily Series**

Lyssa's Destruction Book 1

https://goo.gl/CQ5fzD

Lost Souls of Brunswick Book 1.5

http://myBook.to/Brunswick

**Conjuring Chaos Series**

Chaos and Burnt Offerings Book 1

http://myBook.to/ChaosAndBurntOfferings

Shivers Book 2 (with Donna Owens and Betsy Pfaller)

http://mybook.to/GetShivers

**Dragon's of Death MC Series**

Depraved Retribution Book 1

http://myBook.to/DepravedRetribution

Immoral Retribution Book 2

Coming July 2019

**Dank Series**

Dank: The Evolution of A Clown

http://mybook.to/Dank

Dank: Evolved

Ssshhh....its a secret

A THANK YOU NOTE

***Thank you:***

To my amazing PA Shanna Blanton. Couldn't imagine doing this without her!

To my newest PA for The Horror Authors Carnival, Anibet Castro-Mangual, for being so perfect and helping in my time of need.

To my kick ass editor Ed Bar. He wanted to strangle me and kick me, but along the way, we made it! (Good thing he loves me!)

To my two amazing proofreaders, Marylou Arriaga and Lindsay Crook, for insuring that I dotted all my **T**s and crossed all my **I**s.

To Dez Purington of Pretty In Ink Creations for this brilliant cover!

To my group, Emery's Chaos Crematorium and

my pimp group, Emery's Pimp Shit, couldn't do this without you!

Last, but certainly not least, thank you to the beautiful kick ass ladies of the Inferno World for letting me be part of their journey and allowing me to play! Fucking adore them all!

ABOUT THE AUTHOR

Emery LeeAnn is an international bestselling author who lives in Ohio with her family. Besides being addicted to coffee, she is a true believer that variety adds spice to your life. Writing in every genre gives her the variety she craves. Her characters like to invade her mind every hour of the day, usually waking her up in the middle of the night. Loving the dark and gray side of things, she is exploring her passion with the written word. There are many wonders to come from her twisted Wonderland… Stick around, you may find you enjoy her special brand of torture.

Printed in Great Britain
by Amazon